The Country Bunny

AND THE LITTLE GOLD SHOES

We HEAR of *the* Easter Bunny who comes each Easter Day before sunrise to bring eggs for boys and girls, so we think there is only one. But this is not so. There are really *five* Easter Bunnies, and they must be the five kindest, and swiftest, and wisest bunnies in the whole wide world, because between sunset on Easter Eve and dawn on Easter Morning they do more work than most rabbits do in a whole year.

When one of the Easter Bunnies grows old and can no longer run fast, the old, wise, and kind Grandfather Bunny who lives at the Palace of Easter Eggs calls the bunnies together from the whole world to select the very best one to take the place.

Often a mother bunny says to her child, "Now if you learn to be wise, and kind, and swift, some day you may grow up to be one of the Easter Bunnies." And all of the babies try their very best, so that they can grow up and go to work for the Grandfather Bunny at the Palace of Easter Eggs.

One day a little country girl bunny with a brown skin and a little cotton-ball of a tail said, "Some day I shall grow up to be an Easter Bunny: — you wait and see!"

Then all of the big white bunnies

who lived in

fine houses,

The Country Bunny

AND THE LITTLE GOLD SHOES

AS TOLD TO JENIFER

By DuBose Heyward
Pictures by Marjorie Flack

HOUGHTON MIFFLIN COMPANY

BOSTON

ISBN 0-395-15990-3 (rnf.)
ISBN 0-395-18557-2 (pbk.)

Printed in Malaysia

TWP   75 74 73 72 71
4500310316

and the Jack Rabbits with long legs who can run so fast,

laughed at the little Cottontail and told her to go back to

the country and eat a carrot. But she said, "Wait and see!"

The little girl Cottontail grew up to be a young
lady Cottontail. And by and by she had a husband
and then one day, much to her surprise there
were twenty-one

Cottontail babies

to take care of.

Then the big white rabbits and the Jacks with long legs laughed and laughed, and they said, "What did we tell you! Only a country rabbit would go and have all those babies. Now take care of them and leave Easter eggs to great big men bunnies like us." And they went away liking themselves very much.

Cottontail stopped thinking about hopping over the world with lovely eggs for little boys and girls, and she took care of her babies.

And one day, when her children stopped being babies and were little girl and boy bunnies, she called them to her and said,

"Now we are going

to have some fun."

Then to two of them she gave little brooms

and showed them how to

sweep out the cottage,

and two she taught

how to make beds.

Two more went with her

to the kitchen,

and in no time at all

had found out

how to cook

a good dinner.

And with these went
the two little dish-washers,
and they made the glasses
shine like crystal.

Two had little washtubs
full of soapsuds,
and they washed
all the linen.

Two did the sewing and mending.

Two who had sweet voices were taught to sing

and two more to dance and these amused all the

others while they worked so that they were gay and

happy.

Two others were soon

digging in the garden.

To two she gave paints and crayons,

so they could make pretty pictures

for the walls.

And

when Mother Cottontail had given out all

of the tasks, she looked around, and there

was only one little boy bunny left,

and he was sad and lonely.

Then Mother Cottontail

said to him, "You are the

most polite of all my children

so I shall make you keeper

of my chair. And whenever I come to

dinner you shall seat me politely at table."

Then one day when the little rabbits were half

grown up, she heard a great talk among the woods

rabbits, and when she asked what it was about,

they said, "Haven't you heard? One of the five

Easter Bunnies has grown too slow, and we are

all going to the Palace of Easter Eggs to see Old

Grandfather pick out a new one to take his place."

So she called her little Cottontails and they all
set off to the Palace to see the fun. But their mother
was sad because she thought that now she was
nothing but an old mother bunny, and could only
look on, and that a big handsome white rabbit
or long-legged Jack would be chosen.

When they came to the Palace of Easter Eggs
there were bunnies everywhere on the great lawn,
and the ones that hoped to be the Easter Bunny

stood together, and all the others looked at them
and clapped their paws. Then the big front door
opened and the old, wise, and kind Grandfather
came hopping slowly out. And he told the biggest
and those with the longest legs to show what they
could do. They jumped and ran and showed
him their pretty white fur,

and they were all very fast

and very clever.

But still he did not pick one. And he said to them, "You are pretty and you are fast, but you have not shown me that you are either kind or wise."

Then his kind old eyes looked everywhere and at last they rested on Little Cottontail Mother where she stood with her children around her. And he called her to come right up to the Palace steps. So she took her twenty-one children and went up

and stood before him.

And when he spoke, his voice was so kind that she was not frightened at all. And he said, "What a large family you have, my dear. I suppose they take all of your time."

But she said, "When they were babies, that was so, but now they are so well trained that they do most of the work for me."

"Ah," he said, smiling, "you must be very *wise* to train so many children so well. But tell me, do they always look so happy, and do they always hold their ears up so prettily?"

"Indeed they do," she answered. "We never have a tear or a cross word in our little country cottage. And if I do say it myself, they do carry their ears better than most bunnies."

"Then," he said, patting the nearest bunny on the head, "you must be very *kind* indeed to have such a happy home. It is too bad that you have

had no time to run and grow swift, as I might then

have made you my fifth Easter Bunny."

At that Mother Cottontail started to laugh, then

she whispered to the little bunnies, and every

rabbit on the lawn looked to see what would

happen and the old Grandfather leaned forward

to watch. Suddenly all of her twenty-one children

raced away.

And Cottontail dashed

after them, and

in no time at all

she had them all back

again in front of the Palace

Then the old, kind, wise Grandfather Bunny
said, "I see that you are *swift* also. It is too
bad that you cannot go to carry my eggs,
because you will have to stay at home to
take care of your children."

Mother Cottontail nodded her head to the little ones and they all formed a line and bowed low to the Grandfather. Then she stepped in front of them, and she said, "They will take better care of the house than I."

Then she called them up two by two, and as she put her hands on the heads of each pair she said, "These are my sweepers. They keep the cottage as clean as your hand. These make the beds without a wrinkle. These cook my dinner. These wash the dishes. These tend the garden. These wash and dry all the clothes. These do the mending. These sing, and these dance to keep us merry while we work. These are learning to paint pretty pictures for our walls. And this littlest one of all always pulls out my chair for me when I sit to table. So you see I can leave them to take care of the house until I come home."

Then the old, kind, wise Grandfather said, "You have proved yourself to be not only *wise*, and *kind*, and *swift*, but also very clever. Come to the Palace tomorrow afternoon, for that is Easter Eve,

and you shall be

my fifth Easter Bunny."

The NEXT evening Cottontail knocked on the big
front door and was admitted to the Palace. There
she stood in her funny country clothes but none
of the other four Easter Bunnies laughed, for
they were wise and kind and knew better.

They showed her all over the Palace, from room

to room all piled high with eggs of gold and silver,

and eggs that glittered like snow, chocolate

eggs, marshmallow eggs, eggs for rich children

and eggs for poor children, for children who were

sick and children who were well all over the world.

Then, as soon as it was dark enough for the children to be asleep all over the world, the old, wise, kind Grandfather gave the word and the five bunnies set to work as fast as they could. First one, then another would take up a large egg or a pretty little basket and in a single hop would be out of the Palace and away out of sight. Then in a moment he would be back again, and before you could say Jack Robinson he would have whisked away again.

Slowly the night wore away, and the bunnies began to look tired as they kept returning for more and more eggs. And in the Palace the glittering piles grew smaller and smaller.

Poor little Cottontail was very tired, for this was the first time she had ever gone so far or so fast in her life, and she was beginning to hope that she could soon take the little basket that was set aside for her own children and go hopping home, when old, wise, kind·Grandfather called her to him.

When she went close, she saw that he was holding in his hand the loveliest egg she had ever seen. It glittered like a diamond. "Peek through and see what you shall see," he said; so she peeked through the little hole in one end and she saw a beautiful scene with a sleigh, and a lake with people skating on the ice. And he said, "Because you have such a loving heart for children, I am going to give you the best but the hardest trip of all. Far off over two rivers and three mountains there is a great mountain peak. And in a little cottage on that peak is a little boy who has been ill for a whole year, and who has been so brave that never once has he cried or complained. The mountain is so high that there is ice on the top, and it will be hard to climb, but if you get there you will give more happiness than any other Easter Bunny."

Cottontail picked up the egg very gently and went hopping away on her journey.

She crossed the first river and then the

second. She went over the first

mountain and then

another mountain

and yet another until

at last she reached

the highest mountain of all.

She was very tired when at last she got to the

bottom of the great peak, and her heart failed her

when she saw how high it was,

and how slippery with ice

and snow on top. But,

holding the egg

very carefully, she started hopping up. At last

she reached the ice and snow and now she was

almost to the top and she could see the little

cottage all covered with snow where the little boy

was sleeping. Then a terrible thing happened.

Her foot slipped and down she came — down-

ward she flew into snowdrifts. Then she left the

ice and snow and rolling and bouncing against the

stones she felt the air getting warmer.

Down, down she went, and she crashed through a thicket of budding laurel, rolled across a pasture, and finally struck against the trunk of a great apple tree that was just getting ready to bloom for Easter. And there she lay, with the egg still safely clutched in her paw, but with a great pain in her leg.

She tried to rise again, because she saw a lovely pink light in the sky and she knew that in a few minutes more it would be day, and the little boy would be sad if she did not get his egg to him. But the pain was so bad she fell down. Then she felt something touch her shoulder, and she looked up, and there, right before her, way off there in

that distant land, was old, wise, kind Grandfather Bunny.

And he smiled at her and he said, "You are not only *wise*, and *kind*, and *swift*, but you are also the *bravest* of all the bunnies. And I shall make you my very own Gold Shoe Easter Bunny." And he reached over and she saw for the first time that he was holding a tiny pair of gold shoes in his hand. And he bent down and put them on her feet. Suddenly all the pain left her leg, and she stood up and picked up the precious egg. Then, before she knew what was happening, she felt a sudden motion, and she found herself

flying high in the air: over

the pasture she flew,

over the laurel, over the stones, until at last, when

she landed, she looked back and she saw that one

single jump had carried her halfway up the

mountain. Then she jumped once again and there

she was at the cottage door.   Quickly she squeezed

through the tiny crack that had been left open

just in case the bunny did come all that way, and

in the hand of the beautiful sleeping boy, she

placed the egg.

Then, just as the Easter Morning sun rose over

the edge of the world, she jumped quickly back

to the Palace, where she found

her little basket

for her own little bunnies, and went hopping back home to give them a happy Easter.

Mother Cottontail found that the garden was tended.

And sure enough, just as she had said, everything was in order. The floors were swept and there were two lovely new pictures painted and hanging on the wall.

The dishes were washed and shone in the cupboard.

The clothes were washed and mended and nicely hung away. And

the little house of Mother Cottontail can always
be told now from the homes of all other bunnies.
Because in a special place on the wall, on a
very special hook, hangs a pair of very tiny
little gold shoes.

her twenty-one children were all sound asleep in
their little beds.

And